Per i Professori BONICHI e GRECO, e per le loro preziose lezioni al Liceo Michelangelo, Firenze.

Library of Congress Cataloging-in-Publication Data is available.

Library of Congress Catalog Card Number 2002019218

FIRST U.S. edition 2002

ISBN 0-7636-1907-8

1 2 3 4 5 6 7 8 9 10   PRINTED IN CHINA

This book was hand lettered by the author.

The illustrations were done in collage.

CANDLEWICK PRESS 2067 Massachusetts Avenue

CAMBRIDGE, MASSACHUSETTS 02140

visit us at www.candlewick.com

for DAVID (P.) ♥

SARA FANELLI

MYTHOLOGICAL MONSTERS

OF ANCIENT GREECE

WATCH OUT FOR THEIR HUGE TEETH.
BEWARE THEIR MANY HEADS.
COUNT THEIR EYES.
IMAGINE THEIR POWERS...

IF YOU DARE!

CANDLEWICK PRESS
CAMBRIDGE, MASSACHUSETTS

ARGUS

AFTER HIS DEATH, the GODDESS HERA PUT HIS EYES ONTO the TAIL FEATHERS OF the PEACOCK.

The MONSTER WITH 100 EYES.

EVEN WHEN HE WAS SLEEPING, HE NEVER CLOSED MORE THAN 2 EYES AT ONCE.

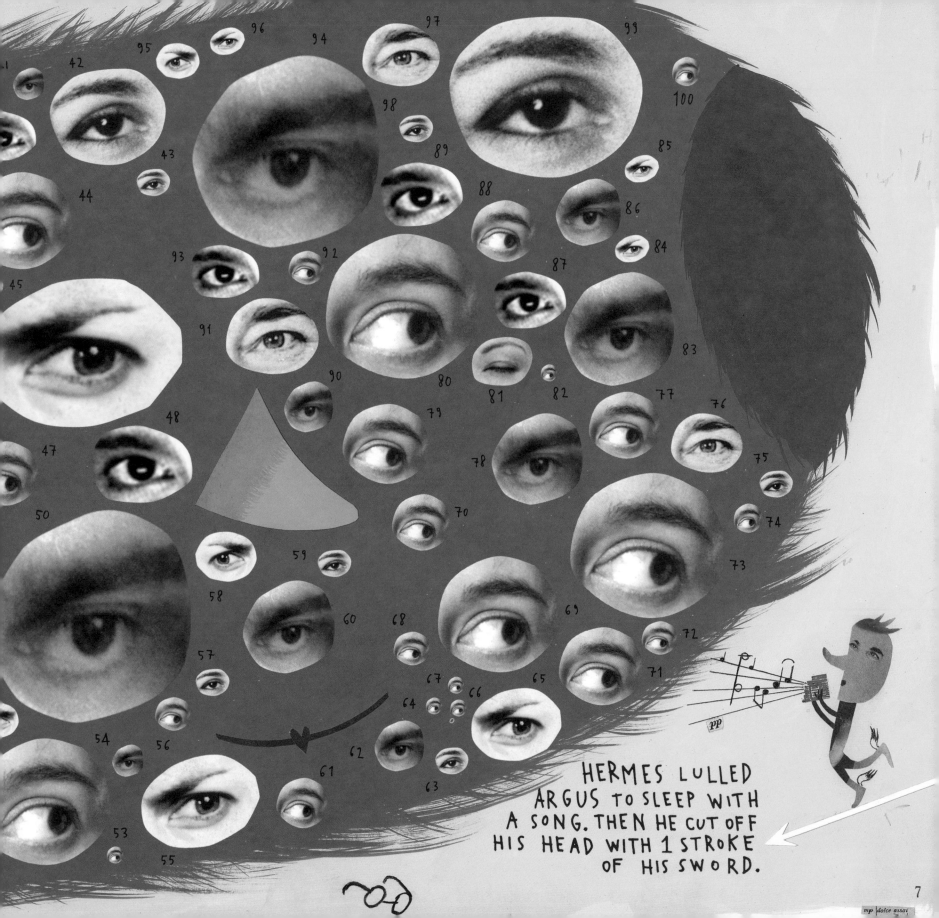

HERMES LULLED ARGUS TO SLEEP WITH A SONG. THEN HE CUT OFF HIS HEAD WITH 1 STROKE OF HIS SWORD.

CLEVER PERSEUS KILLED
MEDUSA. HE LOOKED AT
HER REFLECTION IN HIS
SHINY SHIELD AND
NEVER ONCE GLANCED INTO
HER DEADLY EYES.

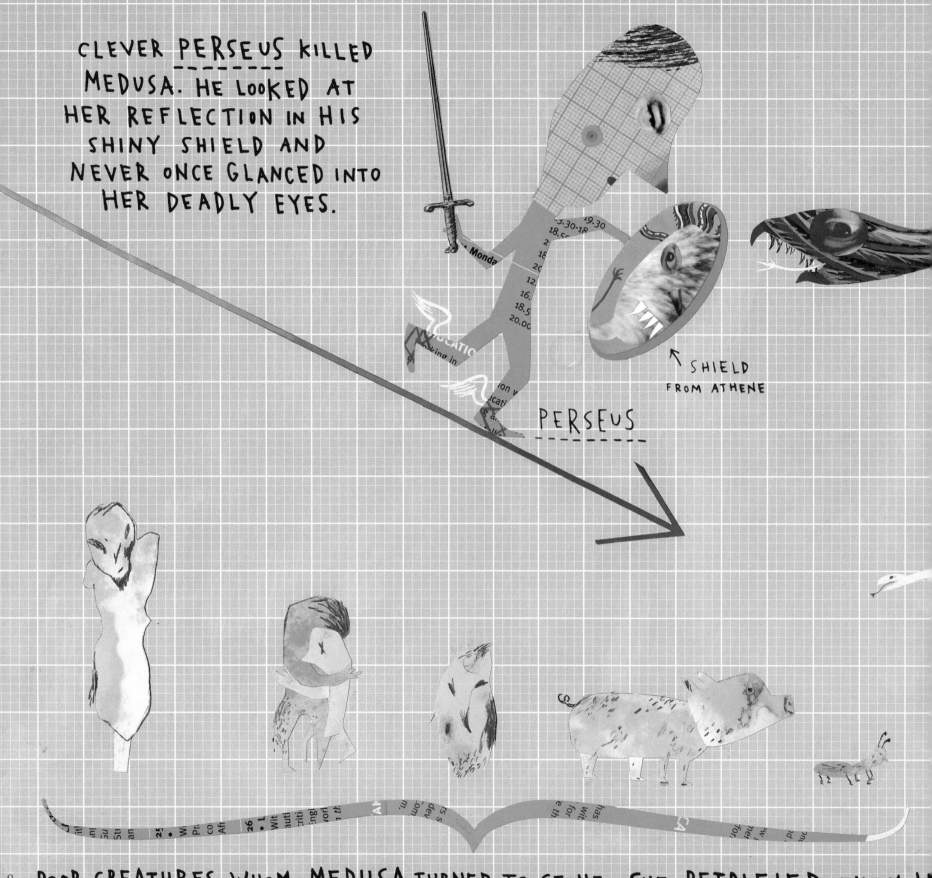

SHIELD
FROM ATHENE

PERSEUS

POOR CREATURES WHOM MEDUSA TURNED TO STONE. SHE PETRIFIED THEM !!

← SNAKES FOR HAIR!

MEDUSA

THE GORGON WHOSE TERRIBLE EYES COULD TURN A PERSON TO STONE.

GORGON

S
E
STHENO EURYALE
→ MEDUSA'S 2 GORGON SISTERS

PEGASUS

The **WINGED** HORSE OF the MUSES*
WAS BORN FROM the BLOOD OF MEDUSA WHEN SHE
WAS KILLED BY PERSEUS.

ONE OF PEGASUS' TASKS
← WAS CARRYING
LIGHTNING BOLTS TO
ZEUS.

FRAGILE ⇈

PEGASUS CARRIED BELLEROPHON
IN HIS BATTLE WITH THE
FIRE-BREATHING CHIMAERA.

brave

pp

(LATE JOBSON AND CO)

***9** GODDESSES WHO INSPIRED ARTISTS, MUSICIANS, SCIENTISTS, AND POETS.

← BELLEROPHON

P

MOUNT HELICON

THE CHIMAERA

THEY CHARMED PASSING SAILORS WITH THEIR BEAUTIFUL SONGS. THE SIRENS HALF WOMEN, HALF VULTURES

12

ALWAYS SHRIEKING!

FEATHERS AS TOUGH AS ARMOR

BAD BREATH

ALWAYS HUNGRY!

THE HARPIES
SHRIEKING, GREEDY BIRDS WITH WOMEN'S HEADS

13

SCYLLA

CHARYBDIS' ROCK
↓
The MONSTER CHARYBDIS WAS SCYLLA'S NEIGHBOR.

The ROCK BETWEEN ITALY and SICILY WHERE SCYLLA LIVED.

12 FEET
6 HEADS
6 NECKS
6 MOUTHS
(EACH WITH 3 ROWS OF TEETH)

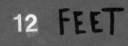

THE SEA MONSTER WITH the UGLY TEMPER WHO GOBBLED UP ALL the SAILORS WHO DARED TO SAIL PAST HER.

16

POLYPHEMUS, A FAMOUS CYCLOPS, KEPT ODYSSEUS AND HIS MEN PRISONER IN HIS CAVE.

ODYSSEUS →

THEY ESCAPED BY HIDING UNDER HIS SHEEP.

C L O P S

KING MINOS

CRETE

EVERY YEAR the
KING of ATHENS
WAS FORCED TO SEND
A TRIBUTE OF
7 YOUNG MEN and
7 MAIDENS
TO BE SACRIFICED
TO the MINOTAUR!

THESEUS

THESEUS SLEW
the MINOTAUR and
ESCAPED FROM
the LABYRINTH with
the HELP of ARIADNE,
MINOS' DAUGHTER.
SHE GAVE THESEUS
A STRING TO
FOLLOW TO FIND
HIS WAY OUT.

Ariadne

LABY

18

THE MINOTAUR

HALF MAN, HALF BULL,
HE WAS KEPT BY KING MINOS OF CRETE
INSIDE A LABYRINTH FROM WHICH
NO ONE COULD ESCAPE.

ICARUS

RINTH (designed by) DAEDALUS

ORPHEUS
SANG CERBERUS TO SLEEP
SO HE COULD SNEAK INTO HADES.

20

CERBERUS

THE 3-HEADED WATCHDOG
WHO GUARDED the GATES OF
HADES, the UNDERWORLD.
HE ONLY ALLOWED
the DEAD TO ENTER.

3

HERACLES
OVERPOWERED CERBERUS AND
DRAGGED HIM UP TO the OVERWORLD.

CENTAURS

HALF MAN, HALF HORSE

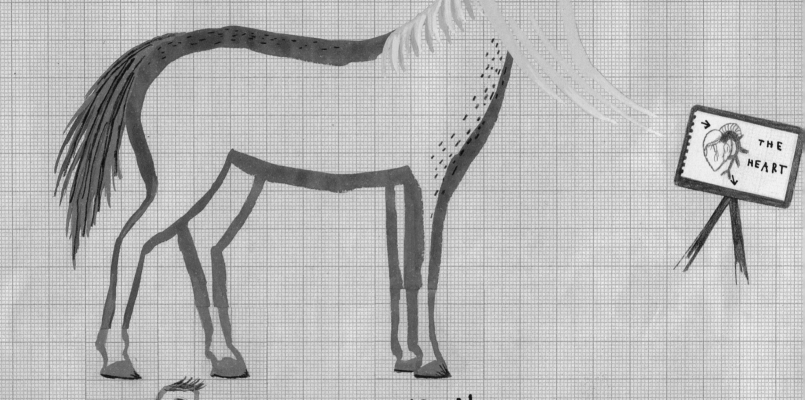

THE HEART

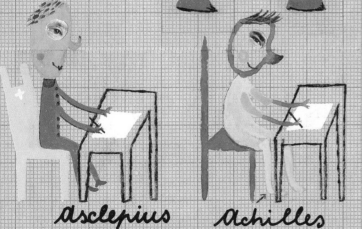

asclepius   *Achilles*

CHIRON'S FAMOUS PUPILS

CHIRON, the CENTAUR, WAS FAMOUS FOR HIS TEACHING.
AFTER HE DIED ZEUS TURNED HIM INTO the CONSTELLATION CALLED SAGITTARIUS. →

SATYRS

HALF MAN, HALF GOAT

THEY WERE FOLLOWERS OF
DIONYSUS, GOD OF WINE,
AND LIVED IN WOODS AND
MOUNTAINS, SINGING AND
PLAYING AND HAVING A
GRAND OLD TIME.

DIONYSUS

IMMORTAL

FIERY BRAND

(TO KEEP DOWN the IMMORTAL HEAD)

ROCK

HERACLES
SLEW the HYDRA
BY BURNING OFF
HER TERRIBLE
HEADS with
A FIERY BRAND.
HE BURIED HER
IMMORTAL
HEAD
UNDER A HUGE
ROCK.

HERACLES

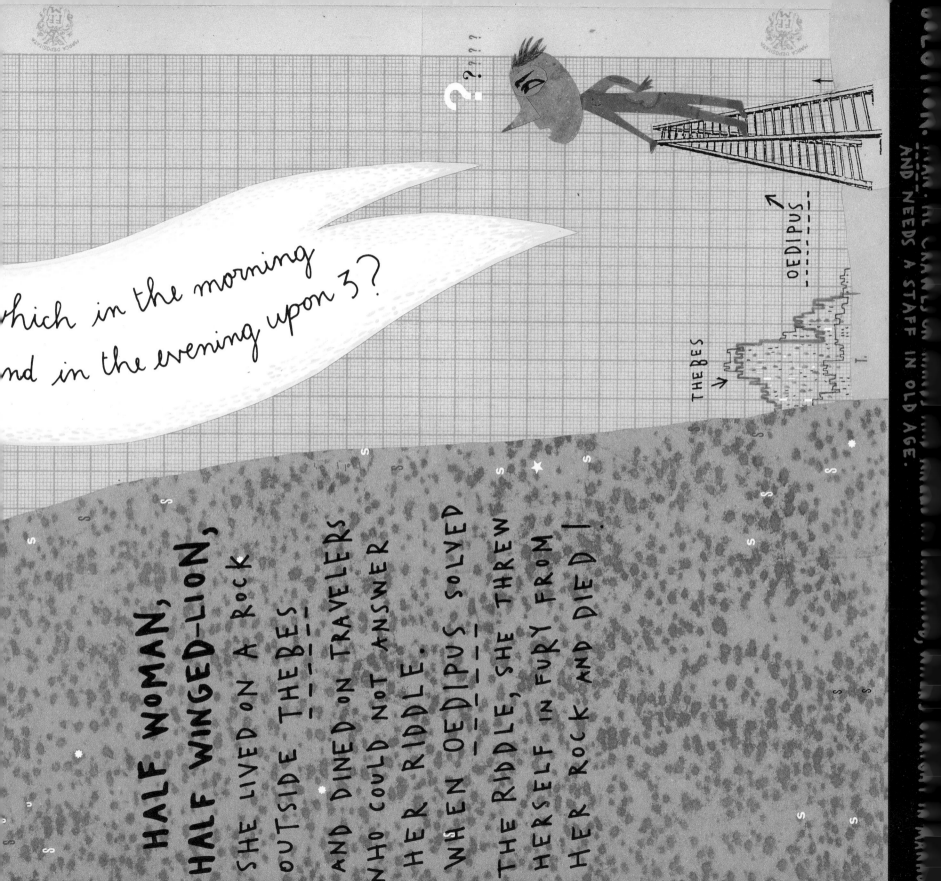

which in the morning
and in the evening upon 3?

OEDIPUS

THEBES

HALF WOMAN,
HALF WINGED-LION,

SHE LIVED ON A ROCK
OUTSIDE THEBES

AND DINED ON TRAVELERS
WHO COULD NOT ANSWER
HER RIDDLE.

WHEN OEDIPUS SOLVED

THE RIDDLE, SHE THREW
HERSELF IN FURY FROM
HER ROCK AND DIED!

ECHIDNA
AND HER MONSTROUS CHILDREN!

the HYDRA

CERBERUS

the CHIMAERA

ORTHUS,
the 2-HEADED
DOG

SCYLLA

HALF WOMAN, HALF SERPENT

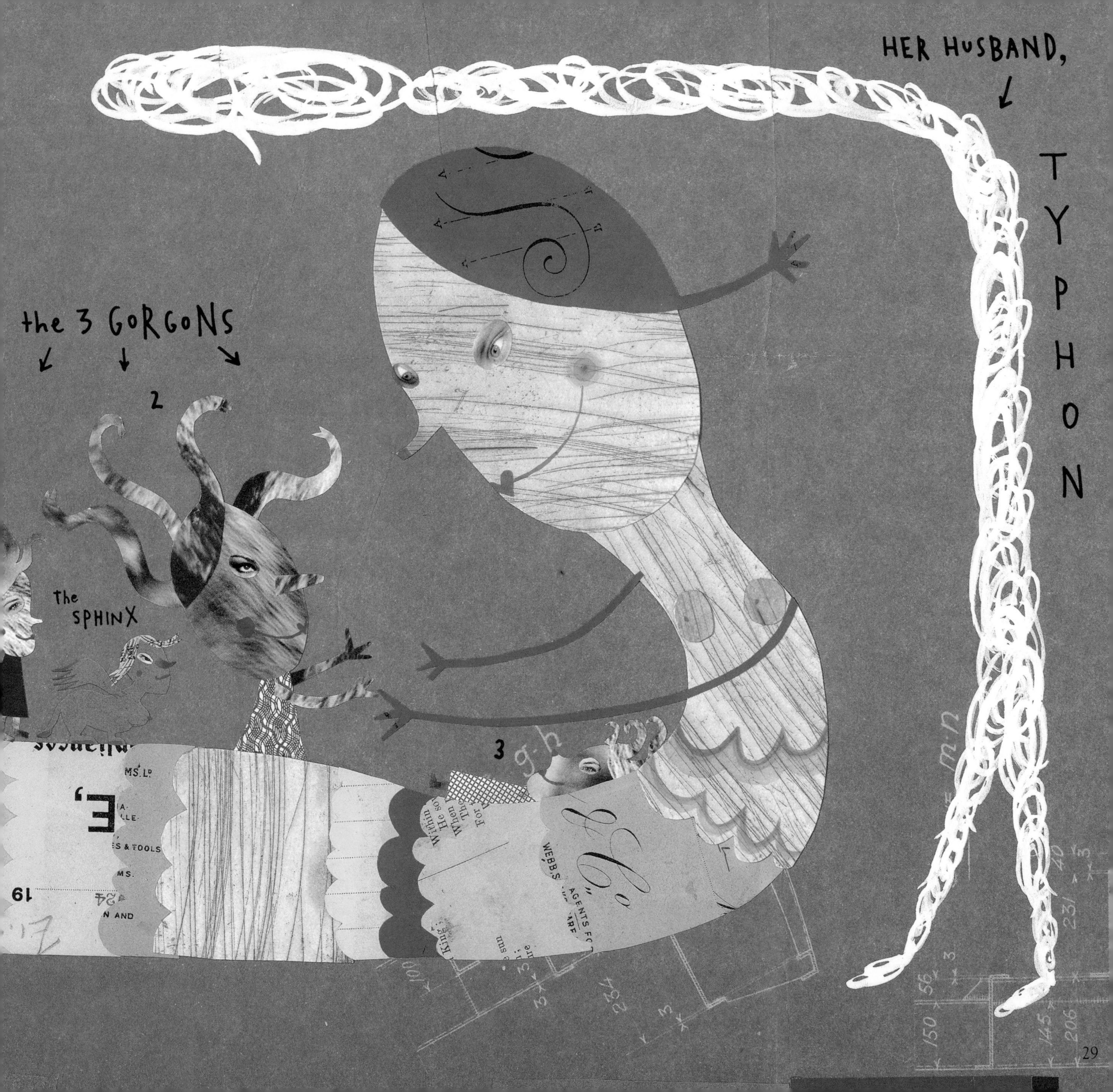

the 3 GORGONS

2

The SPHINX

3

HER HUSBAND,

TYPHON

29

MYTHOLOGICAL MONSTERS

(OF ANCIENT Greece)

↑ WHOSE STRING IS THIS?

ARGUS 6
Argus killed the monster Echidna in her sleep.

MEDUSA 8
Medusa was once beautiful but she insulted the goddess Athene, who became her sworn enemy. First Athene turned Medusa into a frightful creature. Then Athene helped Perseus to kill Medusa by giving him a brightly polished shield and advice on how to avoid her deadly eyes.

PEGASUS 10
Bellerophon killed the Chimaera with the help of Pegasus, and together they carried out many more brave deeds. But when Bellerophon tried to fly Pegasus to Mount Olympus, where only the gods could go, Zeus made Pegasus toss Bellerophon back to Earth. Pegasus then became the carrier of lightning bolts for Zeus.

SIRENS 12
The Sirens' song so enchanted sailors that the men threw themselves toward the Sirens and were drowned. To sail past them safely, Odysseus ordered his sailors to plug their ears with wax. He had himself tied to the mast of his ship so he could hear their songs but not be enchanted by them.

HARPIES 13
One myth about the Harpies describes how they tormented Phineus, a blind soothsayer. The Harpies stole his food, and he almost starved to death.

SCYLLA 14
Though she had six mouths and could seize six sailors in one swoop, Scylla could only yelp or whimper like a newborn puppy.

CYCLOPS 16
According to the Greek writer Homer, the ancestors of the Cyclopes made lightning bolts for Zeus. But they lost this skill and became lawless shepherds who loved to dine on human flesh.

MINOTAUR 18
The string given to Theseus by Ariadne was given to her by Daedalus, the craftsman who made the labyrinth. Because he had offended King Minos and was frightened of him, Daedalus made feather wings so he and his son, Icarus, could escape from the island of Crete. But Icarus flew too close to the sun. Its heat melted the wax that held his wings. He fell into the sea and drowned.

CERBERUS 20
Orpheus charmed his way past Cerberus into the underworld in order to seek his wife, Eurydice. He won permission for her to return to life but only if he did not look at her on their journey back to the overworld.

CENTAURS 22
Chiron's famous pupil Achilles fought at the side of Odysseus in the Trojan War. Asclepius learned the art of healing from Chiron, and so he became the god of medicine.

SATYRS 23
According to the myths, Dionysus and an army of Satyrs wandered all over the world. They scared people with their wild ways, but they also brought with them the knowledge of wine.

HYDRA 24
Killing the Hydra was one of the twelve labors (or tasks) given to Heracles by Hera.

SPHINX 26
Oedipus became the King of Thebes as a reward for freeing the city from the Sphinx. This Sphinx is not the same as the Egyptian Sphinx.

ECHIDNA 28
Echidna's husband, Typhon, tried to kill Zeus. After an immense struggle Zeus buried Typhon under Mount Etna. The sparks from this volcano today are said to be signs that he is still there, trying to escape.

WHO LIVES IN THE
← UNDERWORLD?